Introduction

The big book of *Yeah! Chinese!* contains various resources, which provides teaching recommendations, strategies, etc. to teach each story and new words.

For teacher's convenience, the big book provides contents as following:

Story's brief introduction helps teachers be familiar with the background of each story beforehand. And teachers can differentiate teaching by expanding more information in details from students' prior knowledge.

Main characters help teachers introduce the main characters to students beforehand and guide students into the story.

Learning objectives are prepared for teachers to set up clear daily goals for students.

New words teaching guides provide teachers with suggestions on the process, strategies and activities of introducing the new words.

Warming up provides suggestions on guiding the students to predict and follow the development of the story.

Story teaching guides provide suggestions and hints to help teachers ask key points of the materials.

Hints such as teaching skills, review activities, classroom management methods, culture elements and the fun points of the stories will help teachers to prepare lessons.

Needed videos (with the logo ▶) during teaching can be found on the official website.

How to use Yeah! Chinese! to teach Chinese?

General guidelines for the procedure of a story lesson

If it is a 3 teaching periods per week, it is suggested to teach with following steps: **First period,** teach new words with song and do the activity about the targeted vocabulary. **Second period,** review the new words, song and predict the cover page of the story; and start the new story. **The last period,** do activities about the targeted vocabulary, and retell the story or do a role play. Teachers may do any changes according to class progress.

Ways to teach new words

• Teach action words such as run, catch, take, etc. with body gestures or movements. For example, when introducing the new word "run", the teacher runs at same time.

• Show the flashcards of the new words to establish meaning as an additional visual aid.

• Teach new words with most familiar songs or melodies. For example, when teaching "stand up and sit down", the teacher can sing "stand up and sit down" repeatedly with the "Ten little Indians" melody.

• Use fun activities to help students memorize new words in a low anxiety atmosphere. For example, when teaching the word "bite", ask students to walk around a circle or walk like an animal in the classroom by saying "bite".

Ways to teach story

- Prepare question word cards with Pinyin and English meaning when asking questions. When asking a question, point to the question word to establish the meaning every time.

- Introduce the main characters. e.g. He is Tom. She is Nini. Then ask students what the main characters' names are.

- Start the story from the cover. When asking questions to students, point to the question word to provide clear meaning every time. e.g. What does she say? Who is singing? Is he singing or is she dancing?

- In the middle of the story use 5-wh question words to develop or to bed the story.

- Let students predict the ending. e.g. Who feels hurt? The brother or the sister?

- Sometimes create a pause or wait time to let students finish the sentence or for a tense moment.

- Use sounds and visual tools. Capture students' attention with surprise sound effects. For example, when the students need to say "wow", teach them to use funny sound effect for "wow".

- Maintain eye contact. It will draw students' attention when the teacher makes eye contact with them.

- Use multiple ways of movement. For example, when the students hear the new words such as "be quiet", they need to show "quiet" gesture. As the storyteller, the teacher can "paint" pictures with his / her hands, feet, legs and head.

- Change your voice with different characters. Voice is one of the best ways to bring the character to life and gets students' attention immediately.

- Use props. Don't introduce the props all at once, but bring them out one by one during poignant parts in the telling.

Ways to teach song

- Slow & body movements are the key methods to teach song.

- First of all, let students listen to the melody by demonstrating with body movement.

- The teacher demonstrates singing the song line by line slowly.

- Invite students as a song leader to guide others for singing.

- Sing fast or slow, higher or lower for fun. Let students sing very slowly or sing faster each time to exaggerate the tempo.

- Humming the song. When students are familiar with the song, let them hum the song, which make the song more attractive for them to sing.

- Magic claps or stamp feet. When hearing assigned words, students need to clap hands or "be quiet" or stamp feet. After couple time of practices, then have a competition.

- Play games when singing a song.

Ways to teach games

- Games are played in very class period as a review for the language.
- Model the game before it starts. Invite one or two students to demonstrate how to play the game.
- Explain teacher's expectations before the games.
- Prepare the props or flashcards beforehand for the games.

How to use activities

- Activities are designed to reinforce students' speaking and listening skills.
- Model before starting the activity.
- Prepare the activities with diversified requirements to achieve the maximum benefit of the activity.
- Provide students with more practice in the process by having them share the answers with their partners before answering the class.

Ways to retell a story / do a role play

- Pair up students to retell the story with the retelling page.
- Pair up students. When a student describes the picture randomly, another one points to the picture accordingly.
- Invite students to act out the story either with props or character cards.
- Let students use props or a stage theater to retell the story or do a role play which help some students who are shy to present in low anxiety.

How to use word list

Students themselves can use the word list to review and monitor what they have learned after class. The teacher can use it to check if the students have mastered the words or not. A better way of checking is to combine the word list with flashcards. For example, students should find the correct flashcard when the teacher says a word at random.

Contents

Lesson 1
我头疼
I have a headache

故事简介

教室里有很多小朋友都生病了，有的头疼，有的咳嗽，还有的流鼻涕。小朋友们去护士室，护士发现他们发烧了。

教学目标

1. 掌握常用词语"咳嗽""发烧"和"流鼻涕"。
2. 掌握第三人称代词"他"。

主要人物

Helen

Alan

John

护士

生词教学

- **咳嗽**

1. 领读。（展示图片或动作演示。）
2. 观看视频 ，让学生说一说视频中的动物、人物怎么了。

- **流鼻涕**

1. 领读。（展示图片或动作演示。）
2. 观看视频 ，让学生说一说视频中的人物怎么了。

- **发烧**

1. 领读。（展示图片。）
2. 观看视频 ，让学生说一说视频中的动物怎么了。
3. 课前准备体温计，课上让学生互相量体温，然后告诉大家是否发烧了。

小提示

借助课本 P10 的游戏练习词语。

小提示

借助课本 P12 的活动练习词语。

New words

- 咳嗽
  cough
- 流鼻涕
  running nose
- 发烧
  fever
- 他
  he; him

学过的词：你们、她

• 他

1. 领读。（展示图片。）
2. 借助课本 P9 的歌曲练习词语。

故事热身

提问

1. 他们是谁？（指着图片中的人物一一询问。）
2. 他们在做什么？（指着图片场景询问。）
3. 他们看起来怎么样？（让学生说一说。）

小提示

做小游戏：老师说"你""我"或"他"，然后让学生马上指出来，看谁反应快。

小提示

1. 借助书中的人物图介绍故事主要人物：Alan、Helen、John 和护士。
2. 准备英文图卡解释可能用到的、学生没学过的词语。
3. 提示学生注意 Alan、Helen 和 John 的表情，让学生猜一猜他们怎么了。

提问

1. 她怎么了？（指着 Helen 问。）
2. 你们头疼吗？（让学生说一说。）

小提示

可以带领学生复习表示身体部位的词语。

提问

1. 他怎么了？（指着 Alan 问。）

2. 你们咳嗽吗？（让学生说一说。）

提问

1. 他怎么了？（指着 John 问。）
2. 你们流鼻涕吗？（让学生说一说。）

小提示

提示学生注意 John "流鼻涕"时的表情，让学生说一说他喜欢不喜欢流鼻涕。

提问

1. 谁说"哎呀"？（指着护士问。）
2. 护士为什么说"哎呀"？（让学生猜一猜发生了什么。）

提问

1. 他们怎么了？（指着 Helen、John 和 Alan 问。）
2. 几个人发烧了？（让学生数一数。）

小提示

让学生说一说发烧的小朋友们该做什么。

真臭
Really stinky

故事简介

老虎和小猴子在草地上玩儿的时候闻到了一股臭味儿。它们沿着臭气走向森林深处，路上遇到的小马、小熊和河马都熏得吐了。最后，它们发现，原来是臭鼬放了臭屁。

教学目标

掌握常用词语"放屁"和"吐了"。

主要人物

小马

小熊

河马

臭鼬

生词教学

• 放屁

1. 领读。

2. 观看视频 ▶，让学生说一说视频中的人物怎么了。

3. 借助课本 P21 的歌曲来练习词语。

小提示

借助课本 P22 的游戏做练习。

New words

- 吐了
  threw up
- 放屁
  fart

学过的词：老虎、小马、小鸟、小猴子、真晕、对不起

• 吐了

1. 领读。（展示图片或动作演示。）
2. 观看视频 ▶，让学生说一说视频中的人物怎么了。
3. 借助课本 P21 的歌曲来练习词语。

小提示

借助课本 P23 和 P24 的活动做练习。

故事热身

提问

1. 它们是谁？（指着老虎和小猴子问。）
2. 它们在做什么？（指着老虎和小猴子问。）

小提示

1. 借助书中的人物图介绍故事主要动物：小马、小熊、河马和臭鼬。
2. 准备英文图卡解释可能用到的、学生没学过的词语。

Story

真臭！真臭！

提问

1. 小猴子说什么？（指着小猴子问。）
2. 小鸟为什么飞走了？（让学生猜一猜。）

小提示

提示学生注意臭气飘来的方向。

提问

1. 它是谁？（指着小马问。）
2. 小马怎么了？（指着小马问。）

小提示

提示学生注意小猴子和老虎的动作，让学生说一说小猴子指向什么地方。

提问

1. 它是谁?(指着小熊问。)
2. 小熊怎么了?(指着小熊问。)

小提示

提示学生注意老虎和小猴子的表情和动作,让学生猜一猜它们会对小熊说什么。

提问

1. 它是谁？（指着河马问。）

2. 河马怎么了？（指着河马问。）

小提示

提示学生注意臭气越来越重，天空都变色了，让学生猜一猜为什么。

提问

1. 老虎和小猴子怎么了？（指着老虎和小猴子问。）

2. 它是谁？（指着臭鼬问。）

3. 臭鼬为什么说"对不起"？（指着臭鼬问。）

小提示

1. 引导学生观察图片，注意老虎和小猴子的状态，让学生说猜一猜它们想对臭鼬说什么。

2. 向学生介绍臭鼬什么时候放屁，问问学生是否喜欢臭鼬，是否愿意跟它做朋友。

Lesson 3

我的牙
My teeth

故事简介

教室里学生们有的在看书，有的在玩儿玩具，但是只有 Mary 在急着找东西。原来 Mary 第一次换牙，找不到掉了的牙，所以才那么着急。听到老师的解释和 Bobo 的安慰，Mary 不担心了。

教学目标

1. 掌握常用词语"找""换牙"。
2. 掌握常用疑问代词"什么"。
3. 掌握常用副词"也"。

主要人物

Mary

Bobo

老师

生词教学

• 找
1. 领读。（动作演示。）
2. 借助课本 P33 的歌曲练习词语。

• 什么
1. 领读。（展示图片或动作演示。）
2. 借助课本 P33 的歌曲练习词语。
3. 借助课本 P36 的活动练习词语。

• 换牙
1. 领读。（展示图片。）
2. 观看视频 ▶，让学生说一说视频中的人物怎么了。
3. 借助课本 P35 的活动练习词语。

小提示

准备一些图卡（动物、食物、颜色等），然后将学生分组。每组学生问老师"我们找什么？"，老师随机说目标卡片，最后让学生在有限时间内找出来。

小提示

1. 准备一些情境图片（打球、看书、画画、睡觉），让学生说一说他们想做什么，不想做什么。
2. 可以配合动词"找"做活动。

New words

- 找
  look for
- 什么
  what
- 换牙
  grow new teeth
- 也
  too

学过的词： 我、牙、掉了

- 也

1. 领读。
2. 借助课本 P33 的歌曲练习词语。
3. 借助课本 P35 的活动练习词语。

故事热身

提问

1. 教室里有几个小朋友？（指着图片中的小朋友问。）
2. Bobo 和 Helen 在做什么？（指着 Bobo 和 Helen 问。）
3. 谁在玩儿玩具？（让学生说一说。）

小提示

将学生分组，让每组学生都做相同的活动（踢毽子、跳房子、打球等），然后让做相同活动的学生用"也"说句子。

小提示

1. 借助书中的人物图介绍故事主要人物：Mary、Bobo 和老师。
2. 准备英文图卡解释可能用到的、学生没学过的词语。
3. 提示学生注意小朋友们和老师的表情，让学生说一说他们的表情一样不一样。

提问

Bobo 说什么？（指着 Bobo 问。）

小提示

提示学生注意 Mary 的表情和动作，让学生说一说她在做什么。

提问

老师说什么？（指着老师问。）

提问

1. Mary 怎么了？（指着 Mary 问。）
2. 她掉了几颗牙？（让学生说一说。）

提问

老师说什么？（指着老师问。）

小提示

提示学生注意 Bobo 的表情，让学生想一想 Bobo 为什么笑着点头。

提问

1. Bobo 说什么？（指着 Bobo 问。）
2. 我们班谁换牙了？（让学生说一说。）

小提示

1. 提示学生注意 Bobo 和 Mary 开心的表情，让学生说一说换牙的感受。
2. 可以向学生说明换牙的原因，依照学生的程度，顺带预习生词"长大了"。

我长大了
I'm a grown-up

故事简介

Aiko 一家人在郊外给 Aiko 庆祝五岁生日。爸爸、妈妈领着 Aiko 看到了毛毛虫和小动物的成长，Aiko 也意识到自己长大了。

教学目标

1. 学生能用"我长大了"描述状态。
2. 掌握动物词语"小蝌蚪"和"毛毛虫"。
3. 学生能表达自己的年龄。
4. 学生能用"几岁"询问同辈年龄。

主要人物

Aiko

爸爸

妈妈

生词教学

- **小蝌蚪**

1. 领读。（展示图片。）
2. 观看视频 ，让学生说一说小蝌蚪的成长过程。

- **毛毛虫**

1. 领读。（展示图片。）
2. 观看视频 ，让学生说一说毛毛虫的成长过程。

- **五岁**

1. 领读。（展示图片。）
2. 观看视频 ，让学生说一说视频中的动物、人物几岁了。

小提示

借助课本 P46 的游戏练习词语。

小提示

借助课本 P48 的活动练习词语。

小提示

借助课本 P47 的活动练习词语。

New words

- 我长大了
  I'm a grown-up

- 小蝌蚪
  tadpole

- 毛毛虫
  caterpillar

- 五岁
  five-year old

- 几岁
  how old

学过的词：小鸡

- **几岁**
  1. 领读。（展示图片。）
  2. 观看视频 ▶，说一说视频中的动物、人物几岁了。

小提示
互问互答：让一个学生问"你几岁了？"，然后让另一个学生回答。

- **我长大了**
  1. 领读。
  2. 借助课本 P45 的歌曲练习词语。

小提示
复习"小蝌蚪""毛毛虫"，练习"我长大了"。

故事热身

提问

1. 他们在哪里？（指着 Aiko 一家人问。）
2. 今天是谁的生日？（指着生日卡问，让学生猜一猜。）

小提示
1. 借助书中的人物图介绍故事主要人物：Aiko、爸爸和妈妈。
2. 准备英文图卡解释可能用到的、学生没学过的词语。
3. 提示学生注意 Aiko 一家人的表情，让学生说一说他们开心不开心。

小鸡长大了。

提问

小鸡怎么了？（指着长大的小鸡问。）

小提示

提示学生观察小鸡长大过程中颜色、样子的改变。

提问

1. 这里有几只小蝌蚪？（让学生数一数。）
2. 小蝌蚪怎么了？（指着长大的小蝌蚪问。）

小提示

提示学生观察小蝌蚪长大过程中的改变，让学生说一说它们长大后是什么。

毛毛虫长大了。

提问

1.这里有几只毛毛虫？（指着毛毛虫问。）

2.毛毛虫怎么了？（指着毛毛虫问。）

小提示

1.提示学生观察毛毛虫和蝴蝶的颜色，让学生说一说它们都是什么颜色。

2.提示学生观察毛毛虫成长过程中的改变，让学生说一说它们长大后是什么。

提问

1. Aiko 几岁了？（指着 Aiko 问。）
2. Aiko 长大了吗？（指着 Aiko 问。）

提问

1. Aiko 说什么？（指着 Aiko 问。）

2. 你几岁了？长大了吗？（让学生说一说。）

小提示

让学生说一说自己长大了有什么变化，例如"个子长高了"。